Jack Jump Under
the Candlestick

Donna Lugg Pape
Pictures by Irene Trivas

Albert Whitman & Company, Niles, Illinois

Library of Congress Cataloging in Publication Data
Pape, Donna Lugg.
  Jack jump under the candlestick.
  (Self-starter)
  Summary: Tina exasperates her older brother
by singing nursery rhymes wrong, always substitut-
ing the word under for over.
  [1. English language—Prepositions—Fiction.
2. Brothers and sisters—Fiction] I. Trivas,
Irene, ill. II. Title. III. Series: Self-starter
books.
PZ7.P1978Jac   [E]   82-1918
ISBN 0-8075-3753-5 (lib. bdg.)   AACR2

For Tracy Erin Rickert

I will sing you a song," Tina told her doll.

She sang, "Jack be nimble, Jack be quick, Jack jump under the candlestick."

Her big brother, Eric, said, "You are singing that wrong, Tina."

Eric found a candlestick. He put it on the floor. "I am Jack," he said.

Eric jumped over the candlestick. "See," he said. "It's Jack jump OVER the candlestick."

Tina picked up the candlestick. She held
it over her head. "Now I am Jack," she said.

She jumped and sang, "Jack be nimble, Jack be quick, Jack jump under the candlestick."

"You are silly," Eric said. He jumped
over Tina's doll and went out to play.

Tina played with her wind-up bear.

She sang, "The bear went under the mountain.
The bear went under the mountain.
The bear went under the mountain to see
what he could see."

Eric said, "You are singing that wrong, Tina."
Eric made a mountain with a blanket.
He moved the bear over the blanket.

Eric sang, "The bear went over the mountain.
The bear went over the mountain.
The bear went over the mountain to see
what he could see."

Tina wound up the bear and set it down. Then she made herself into a mountain with a space underneath.

She said, "I am the mountain."

The bear walked under her.

She sang, "The bear went under the mountain.
The bear went under the mountain.
The bear went under the mountain to see
what he could see."

"You are silly," Eric said. He jumped
over the bear and went outside to play.

After supper, Tina sat outside in her
pajamas. She sang, "Hey, diddle, diddle!
The cat and the fiddle, the cow jumped
under the moon."

Eric said, "You are singing that wrong, Tina."
He found a book and showed Tina a picture
of the cow jumping over the moon.

"See," Eric said, "you should sing,
'Hey, diddle, diddle! The cat and the fiddle,
the cow jumped over the moon.'"

Tina pointed to the moon. "I am a cow,"
she said. "Moo, moo."

Then she jumped around the yard and sang,
"Hey, diddle, diddle! The cat and the
fiddle, the cow jumped under the moon."

"You're silly," Eric said. He went into the house.

Soon Tina went inside, too.

"Eric," she called. "Where are you?"

She looked under a chair.

She looked under a pile of clothes.

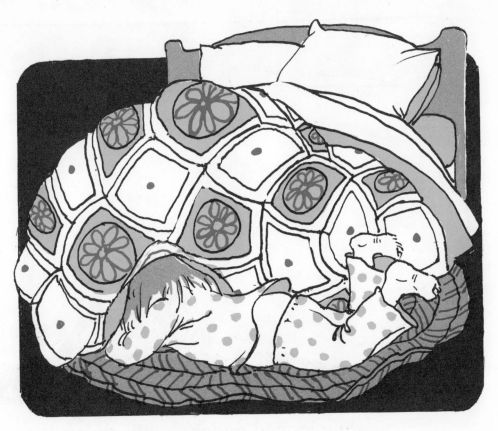

She looked under the beds.

She looked under a table covered
with a long tablecloth.

There was Eric!

He crawled out and said, "Did you look
all over for me?"

Tina laughed and said, "No, I looked all
under for you."

Then she ran into her bedroom, crawled under the covers, and went to sleep.